LIFE IS JUST A CHAIR OF BOWLIES

I love you, you old bear.

To The World
you may be one
PERSON
BUT
TO ONE PERSON
YOU
MAY BE THE
WORLD!

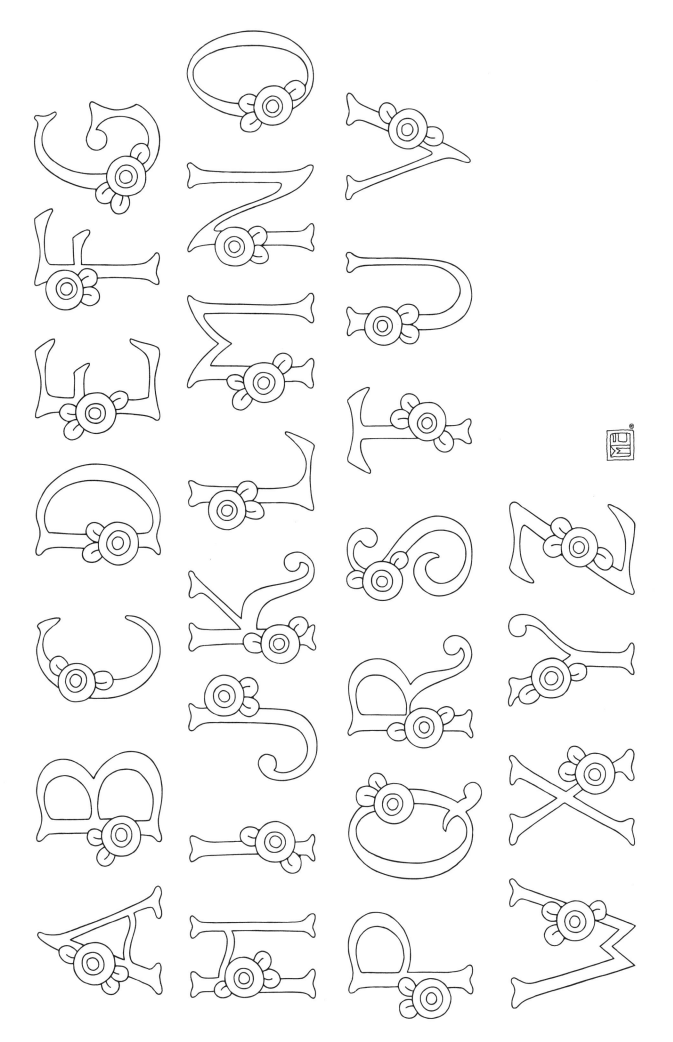

The best teachers are those
who show you where to look,
but don't tell you what to see.

ALEXANDRA K. TRENFOR

THIS IS THE LIFE

YOU ARE

MY HAPPY

GREAT THINGS ARE DONE BY A SERIES OF SMALL THINGS BROUGHT TOGETHER

Vincent Van Gogh

MY TRAIN of THOUGHT DERAILED.

THERE WERE NO SURVIVORS.

Live a life that matters

Live a life of love

YOU MUST ACCEPT WHAT ISN'T, SO THAT YOU CAN MOVE FORWARD WITH WHAT IS

FRIENDS

ARE THE BACON BITS IN THE SALAD BOWL OF LIFE

ME

The ribbons of love are woven around my heart

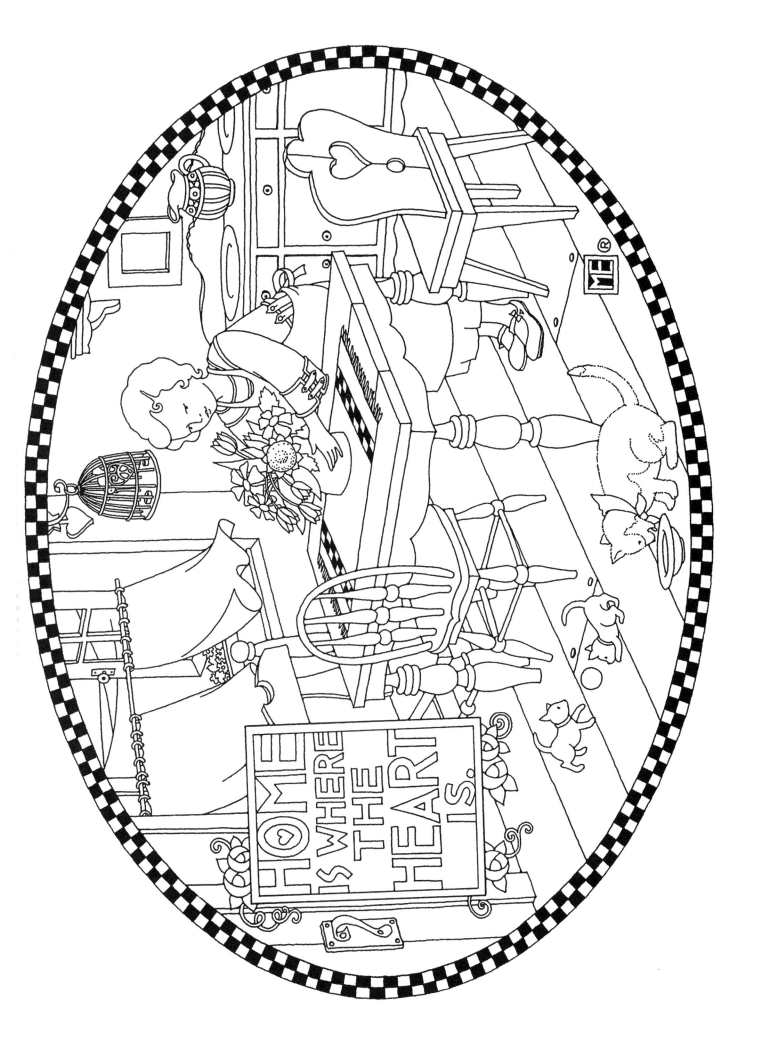

TRAVEL LIGHT
LIVE LIGHT
SPREAD THE LIGHT
BE THE LIGHT